This book belongs to:

_____

_____

Berryland Books

Written by Gill Davies
Illustrated by Eric Kincaid
Edited by Heather Maddock

Published by Berryland Books
www.berrylandbooks.com

First published in 2004
Copyright © Berryland Books 2004

ISBN 1-84577-003-X
Printed in India

Beauty and the Beast

Reading should always be FUN !

Reading is one of the most important skills your child will learn. It's an exciting challenge that you can enjoy together.

Treasured Tales is a collection of stories that has been carefully written for young readers.

Here are some useful points to help you teach your child to read.

Try to set aside a regular quiet time for reading at least three times a week.

Choose a time of the day when your child is not too tired.

Plan to spend approximately 15 minutes on each session.

Select the book together and spend the first few minutes talking about the title and cover picture.

Spend the next ten minutes listening and encouraging your child to read.

Always allow your child to look at and use the pictures to help them with the story.

Spend the last couple of minutes asking your child about what they have read. You will find a few examples of questions at the bottom of some pages.

Understanding what they have read is as important as the reading itself.

Once upon a time there was a rich merchant who had three daughters.

The first two were nasty and selfish, but the third, Beauty, was sweet and kind.

One day the merchant received news that his ships had sunk in a storm.

He was very upset and his two eldest children grumbled because they were now poor.

Beauty never complained and all the work was left to her.

Shortly afterwards, the merchant heard that one of his missing ships had arrived at port and he decided to set off to reclaim it.

He asked each one of his daughters what presents they would like him to bring back.

The eldest two asked for dresses and jewels.

Beauty asked her father for a rose.

What did the two eldest daughters ask for?

By the time the merchant reached the port, he had been robbed of his ship.

Feeling very sad, he began his long journey home back through the forest.

One night there was a heavy snow storm, but the tired man kept on going.

In the distance he saw a castle. He rode up to the gates and stepped inside.

No one was there and the table was laid with a wonderful meal.

He helped himself to some food and then settled down to sleep in a comfortable bed.

The next day he woke up early.

Once again the table was laid with food, so he sat down and enjoyed his breakfast.

Leaving the castle, he walked through a beautiful rose garden.

The roses reminded him of Beauty and he reached out and took one.

Suddenly, an ugly Beast stood before him and roared, "How dare you steal my rose, you shall die!"

"I am very sorry, please forgive me," begged the merchant.

The merchant then told the Beast about his wonderful daughter and her simple request for a rose.

Why was the Beast angry?

"I will let you live if you promise to send Beauty to live with me," said the Beast.

The merchant was not happy, but was afraid to refuse.

He promised and set off home.

"I will be waiting for you," the Beast called out.

When the children saw their father, they all ran out to greet him.

He told them what had happened and he said that Beauty did not need to go.

"You gave your promise, Father, so I must go," replied Beauty.

Beauty felt sad as she did not want to leave her father.

She was afraid of meeting the Beast.

"We shall go together," said her father.

The next day they rode to the castle.

Once again, a beautiful meal was laid out on the table.

They sat down and enjoyed the food.

Why was Beauty sad?

"That was wonderful," Beauty said.

At that moment the Beast appeared in front of them.

Beauty was afraid, but she held out her hand and smiled sweetly.

"Your daughter is very beautiful," said the Beast.

"You must go now but don't worry, I will take good care of her," he said.

Beauty's father said goodbye with a sad heart and went back home.

Beauty soon found that the Beast was very kind and he took good care of her.

As the days went by, Beauty began to like the Beast.

However, she still missed her father very much and this made her sad.

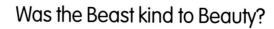
Was the Beast kind to Beauty?

Some nights, while fast asleep, Beauty would have a strange dream.

She dreamt of a kind Prince who told her he was under the spell of a wicked witch.

"The spell can only be broken with a kind and loving heart," he explained.

One day Beauty was feeling very sad and she asked the Beast if she could visit her father.

The Beast agreed but made her promise that she would return.

"If you stay away too long, I will die," the Beast told Beauty.

She promised to be back soon.

Suddenly, Beauty found herself standing outside her home.

Who has Beauty come to see?

Her father was so pleased to see her and wanted her to stay forever.

As the days went by, Beauty found that she was missing the Beast and the Prince in her dreams.

She wanted to go back to the palace.

One night the Beast appeared in Beauty's dream.

He was lying under a tree in the castle grounds looking very sick.

Beauty suddenly remembered the Beast's words.

She knew she had to return.

As she opened her eyes she found herself once more in the castle grounds.

She rushed towards the tree and saw the Beast.

Where is the Beast?

"Oh no!" cried Beauty.

"Please, please wake up.

You are so kind to me and I am here now to look after you," she said.

The Beast opened his eyes.

"Will you marry me, Beauty?" the Beast asked.

For a moment Beauty thought of the Prince in her dreams, but realized he was not real.

Beauty leaned forward and kissed the Beast.

Suddenly, the ugly Beast turned into the handsome Prince of her dreams.

The Prince smiled and said, "Your love has broken the wicked spell."

Beauty was so excited.

"Now we can live together in happiness," she said to the Prince.